SKYLANDERS

THE KAOS TRAP

MINI BUT MIGHTY

Story by:
RON MARZ and **DAVID A. RODRIGUEZ**
Art by:
DAVID BALDEÓN
Colors by:
DAVID GARCIA CRUZ
Letters by:
DERON BENNETT & TOM B. LONG
Edited by:
DAVID HEDGECOCK

Spotlight   IDW

ABDOPUBLISHING.COM

Reinforced library bound edition published in 2016 by Spotlight, a division of ABDO, PO Box 398166, Minneapolis, Minnesota 55439. Spotlight produces high-quality reinforced library bound editions for schools and libraries. Published by agreement with IDW.

Printed in the United States of America, North Mankato, Minnesota.
042015
092015

THIS BOOK CONTAINS
RECYCLED MATERIALS

LIBRARY OF CONGRESS CATALOGING-IN-PUBLICATION DATA

Marz, Ron, author.
  Mini but mighty / writer: Ron Marz and David A. Rodriguez ; artist: David Baldeon ; colors: David Garcia Cruz.
     pages cm. -- (Skylanders: the Kaos trap)
  Summary: "When the students arrive at Skylanders Academy without their pilot, Tessa and Cali search for Flynn. Along the way, they rescue an academy student. Will the girls find Flynn? And what does the student have to do with Kaos?"-- Provided by publisher.
  ISBN 978-1-61479-386-1
  1. Graphic novels. I. Rodriguez, David A., author II. Baldeón, David, illustrator. III. Skylanders (Game) IV. Title.
  PZ7.7.M3754Min 2016
  741.5'973--dc23
                2015001611

Spotlight
A Division of ABDO
abdopublishing.com

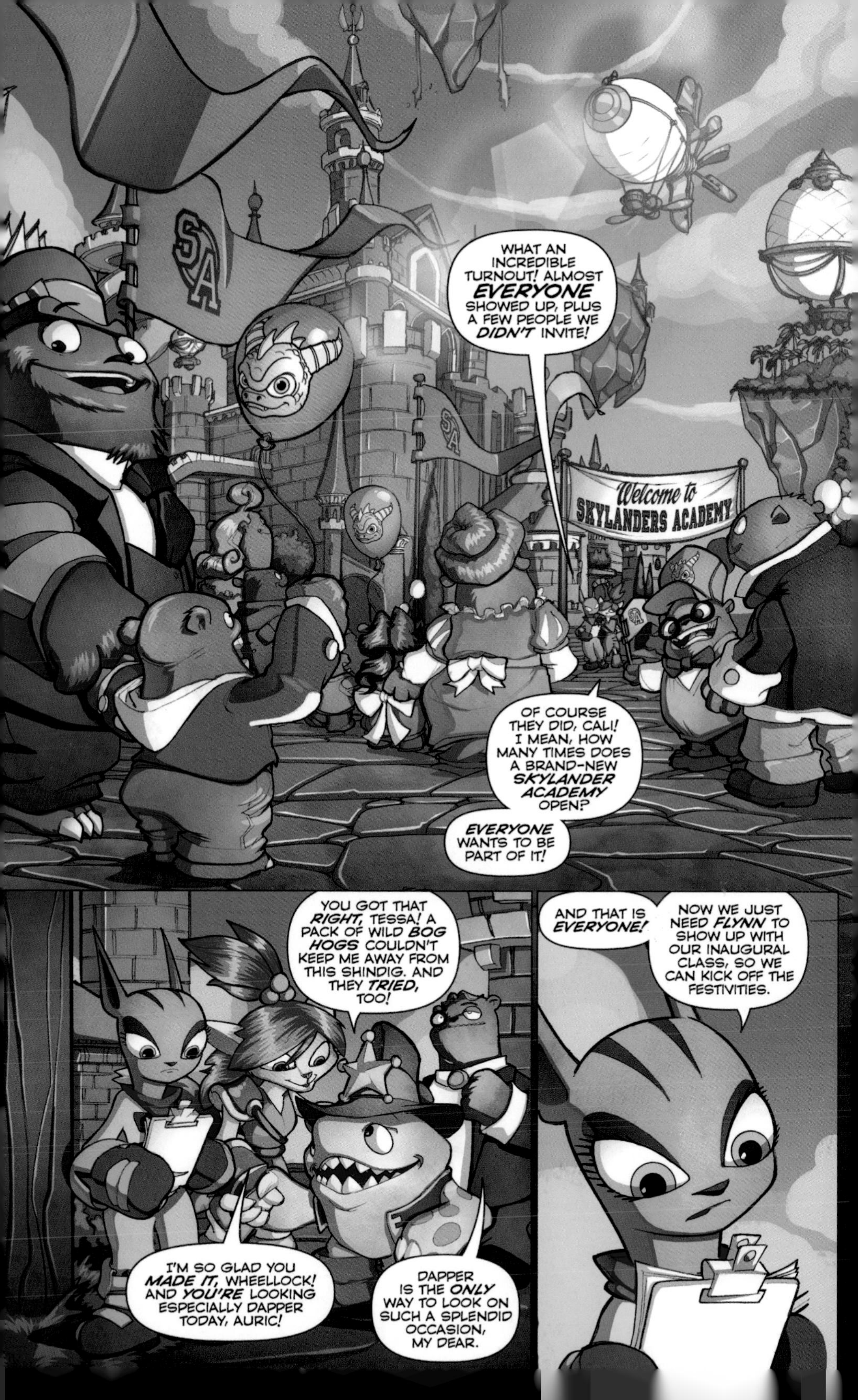
WHAT AN INCREDIBLE TURNOUT! ALMOST EVERYONE SHOWED UP, PLUS A FEW PEOPLE WE DIDN'T INVITE!
Welcome to SKYLANDERS ACADEMY
OF COURSE THEY DID, CALI! I MEAN, HOW MANY TIMES DOES A BRAND-NEW SKYLANDER ACADEMY OPEN?
EVERYONE WANTS TO BE PART OF IT!
YOU GOT THAT RIGHT, TESSA! A PACK OF WILD BOG HOGS COULDN'T KEEP ME AWAY FROM THIS SHINDIG. AND THEY TRIED, TOO!
I'M SO GLAD YOU MADE IT, WHEELLOCK! AND YOU'RE LOOKING ESPECIALLY DAPPER TODAY, AURIC!
DAPPER IS THE ONLY WAY TO LOOK ON SUCH A SPLENDID OCCASION, MY DEAR.
AND THAT IS EVERYONE!
NOW WE JUST NEED FLYNN TO SHOW UP WITH OUR INAUGURAL CLASS, SO WE CAN KICK OFF THE FESTIVITIES.

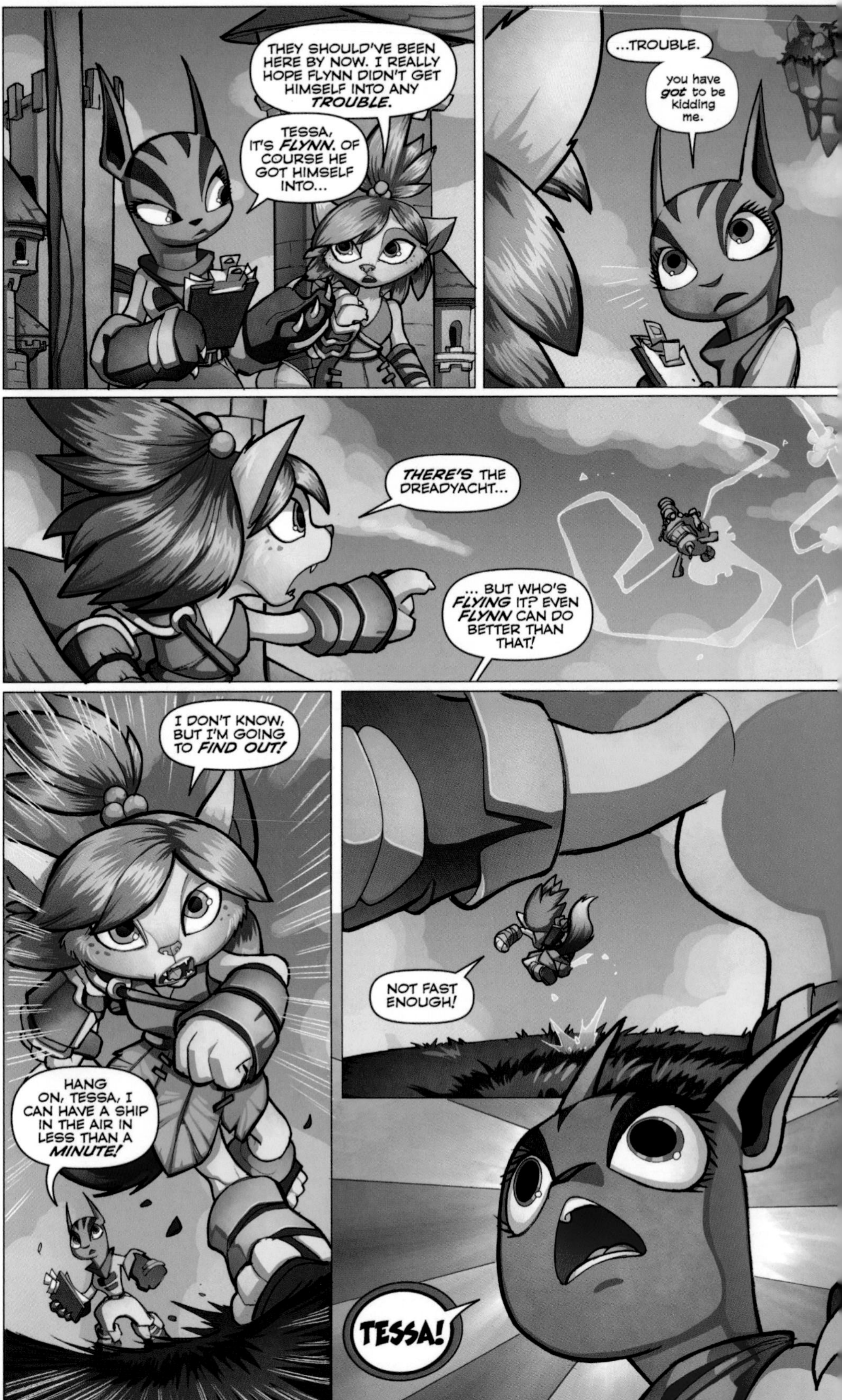
THEY SHOULD'VE BEEN HERE BY NOW. I REALLY HOPE FLYNN DIDN'T GET HIMSELF INTO ANY *TROUBLE.*
TESSA, IT'S *FLYNN.* OF COURSE HE GOT HIMSELF INTO...
...TROUBLE.
you have *got* to be kidding me.
THERE'S THE DREADYACHT...
... BUT WHO'S *FLYING* IT? EVEN *FLYNN* CAN DO BETTER THAN THAT!
I DON'T KNOW, BUT I'M GOING TO *FIND OUT!*
HANG ON, TESSA, I CAN HAVE A SHIP IN THE AIR IN LESS THAN A *MINUTE!*
NOT FAST ENOUGH!
TESSA!

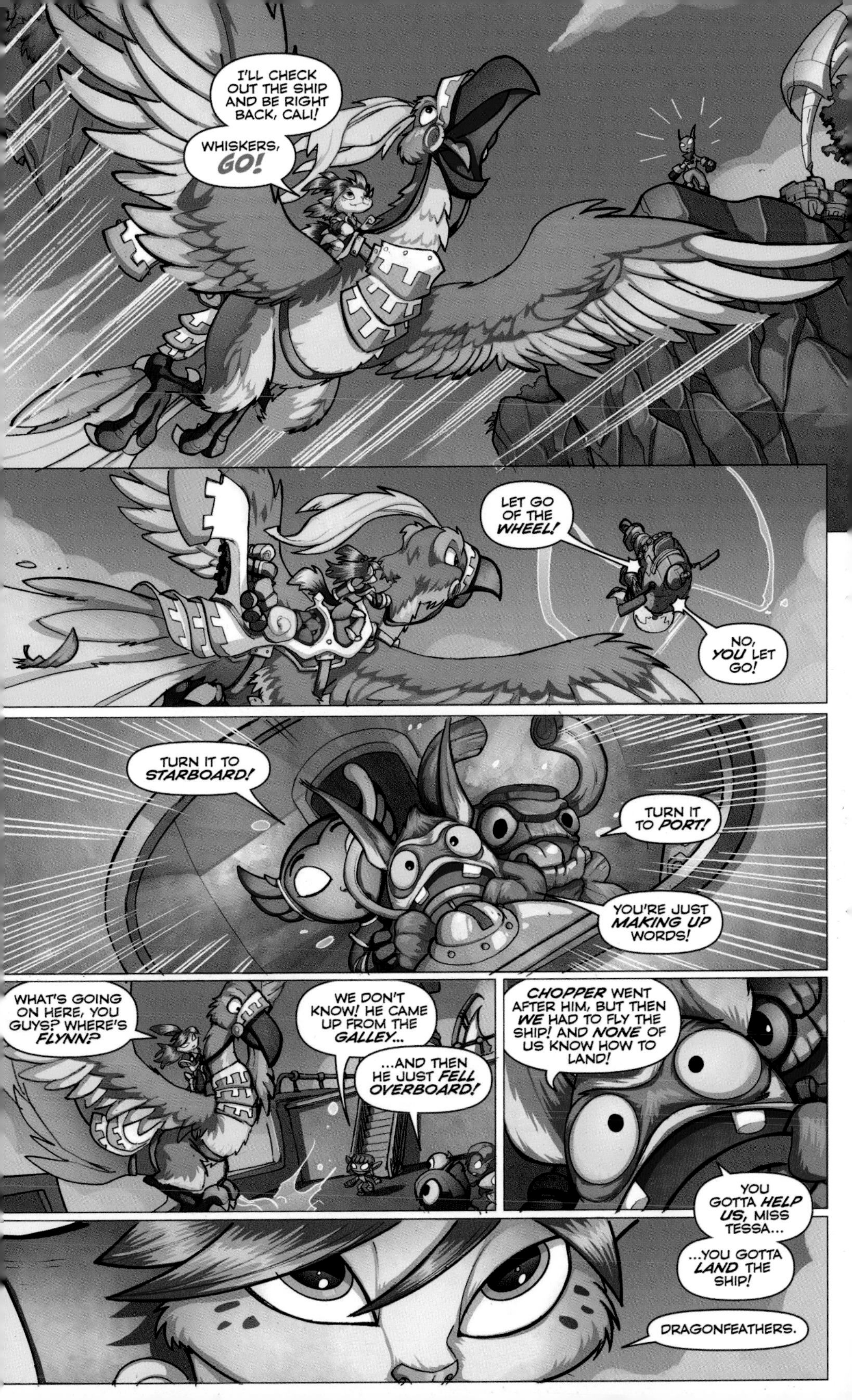
I'LL CHECK OUT THE SHIP AND BE RIGHT BACK, CALI!
WHISKERS, GO!
LET GO OF THE WHEEL!
NO, YOU LET GO!
TURN IT TO STARBOARD!
TURN IT TO PORT!
YOU'RE JUST MAKING UP WORDS!
WHAT'S GOING ON HERE, YOU GUYS? WHERE'S FLYNN?
WE DON'T KNOW! HE CAME UP FROM THE GALLEY...
...AND THEN HE JUST FELL OVERBOARD!
CHOPPER WENT AFTER HIM, BUT THEN WE HAD TO FLY THE SHIP! AND NONE OF US KNOW HOW TO LAND!
YOU GOTTA HELP US, MISS TESSA...
...YOU GOTTA LAND THE SHIP!
DRAGONFEATHERS.

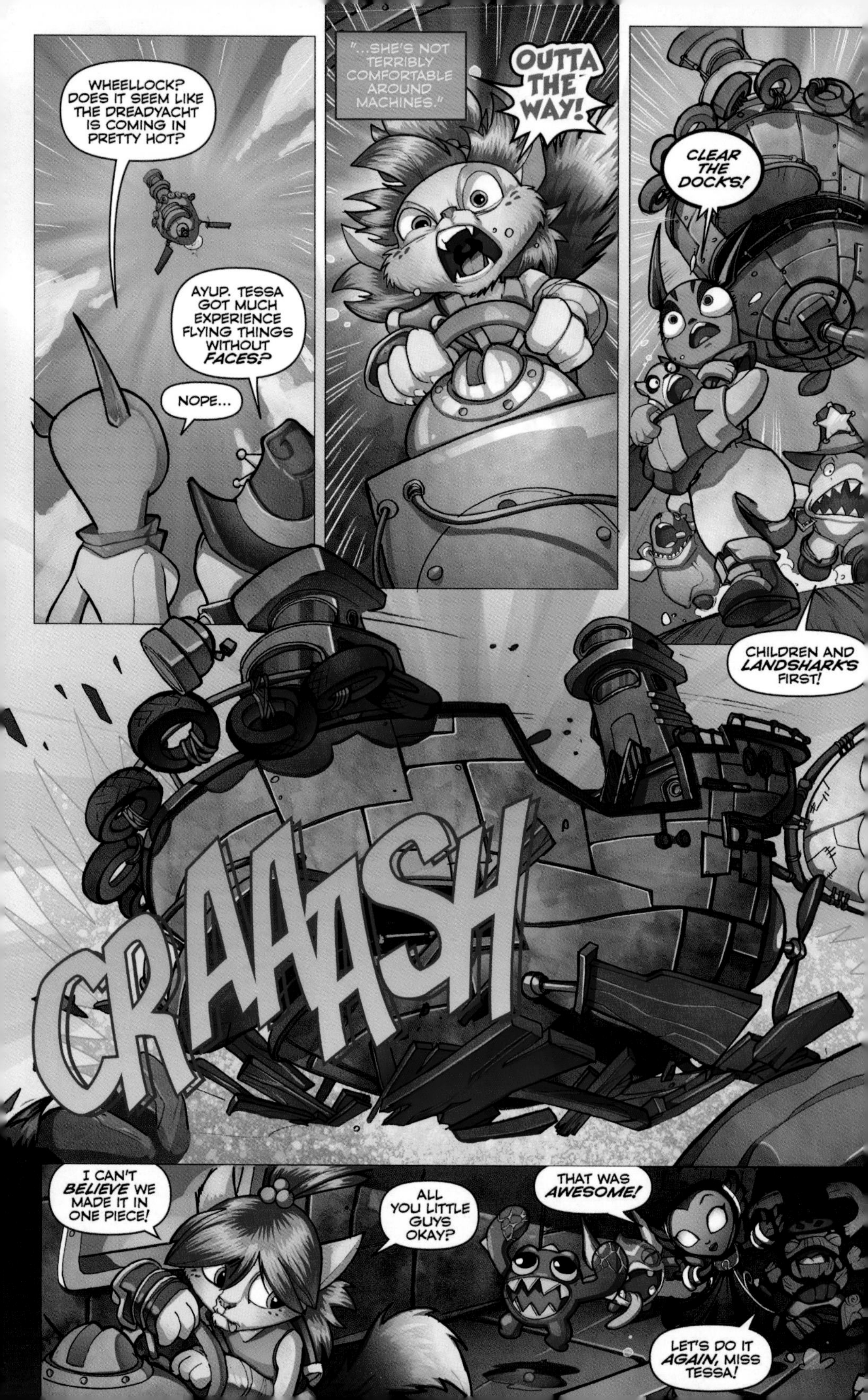
WHEELLOCK? DOES IT SEEM LIKE THE DREADYACHT IS COMING IN PRETTY HOT?
AYUP. TESSA GOT MUCH EXPERIENCE FLYING THINGS WITHOUT FACES?
NOPE...
"...SHE'S NOT TERRIBLY COMFORTABLE AROUND MACHINES."
OUTTA THE WAY!
CLEAR THE DOCKS!
CHILDREN AND LANDSHARKS FIRST!
CRAAASH
I CAN'T BELIEVE WE MADE IT IN ONE PIECE!
ALL YOU LITTLE GUYS OKAY?
THAT WAS AWESOME!
LET'S DO IT AGAIN, MISS TESSA!

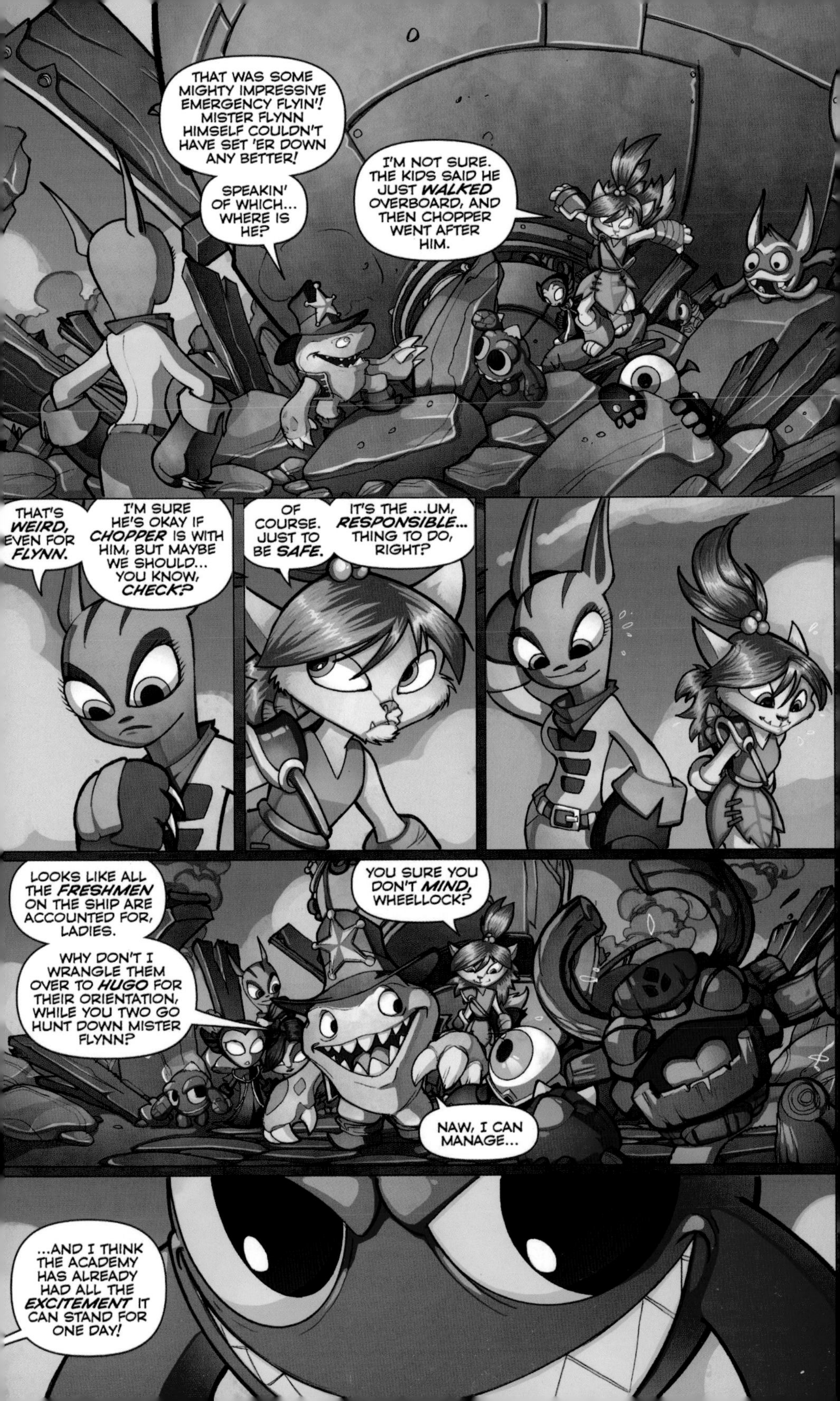
THAT WAS SOME MIGHTY IMPRESSIVE EMERGENCY FLYIN'! MISTER FLYNN HIMSELF COULDN'T HAVE SET 'ER DOWN ANY BETTER!
SPEAKIN' OF WHICH... WHERE IS HE?
I'M NOT SURE. THE KIDS SAID HE JUST WALKED OVERBOARD, AND THEN CHOPPER WENT AFTER HIM.
THAT'S WEIRD, EVEN FOR FLYNN.
I'M SURE HE'S OKAY IF CHOPPER IS WITH HIM, BUT MAYBE WE SHOULD... YOU KNOW, CHECK?
OF COURSE. JUST TO BE SAFE.
IT'S THE ...UM, RESPONSIBLE... THING TO DO, RIGHT?
LOOKS LIKE ALL THE FRESHMEN ON THE SHIP ARE ACCOUNTED FOR, LADIES.
WHY DON'T I WRANGLE THEM OVER TO HUGO FOR THEIR ORIENTATION, WHILE YOU TWO GO HUNT DOWN MISTER FLYNN?
YOU SURE YOU DON'T MIND, WHEELLOCK?
NAW, I CAN MANAGE...
...AND I THINK THE ACADEMY HAS ALREADY HAD ALL THE EXCITEMENT IT CAN STAND FOR ONE DAY!

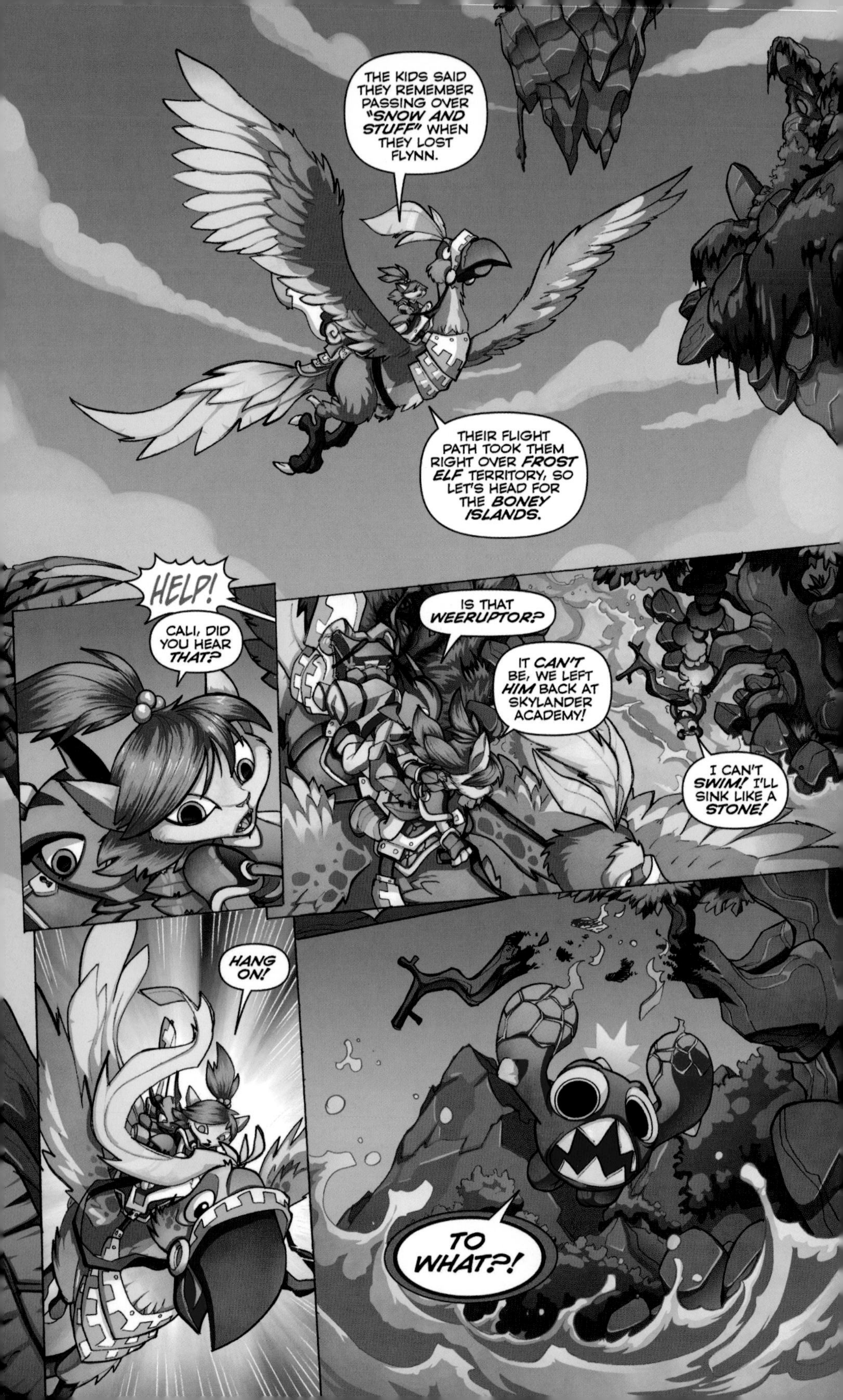

THE KIDS SAID THEY REMEMBER PASSING OVER "SNOW AND STUFF" WHEN THEY LOST FLYNN.
THEIR FLIGHT PATH TOOK THEM RIGHT OVER FROST ELF TERRITORY, SO LET'S HEAD FOR THE BONEY ISLANDS.
HELP!
CALI, DID YOU HEAR THAT?
IS THAT WEERUPTOR?
IT CAN'T BE, WE LEFT HIM BACK AT SKYLANDER ACADEMY!
I CAN'T SWIM! I'LL SINK LIKE A STONE!
HANG ON!
TO WHAT?!

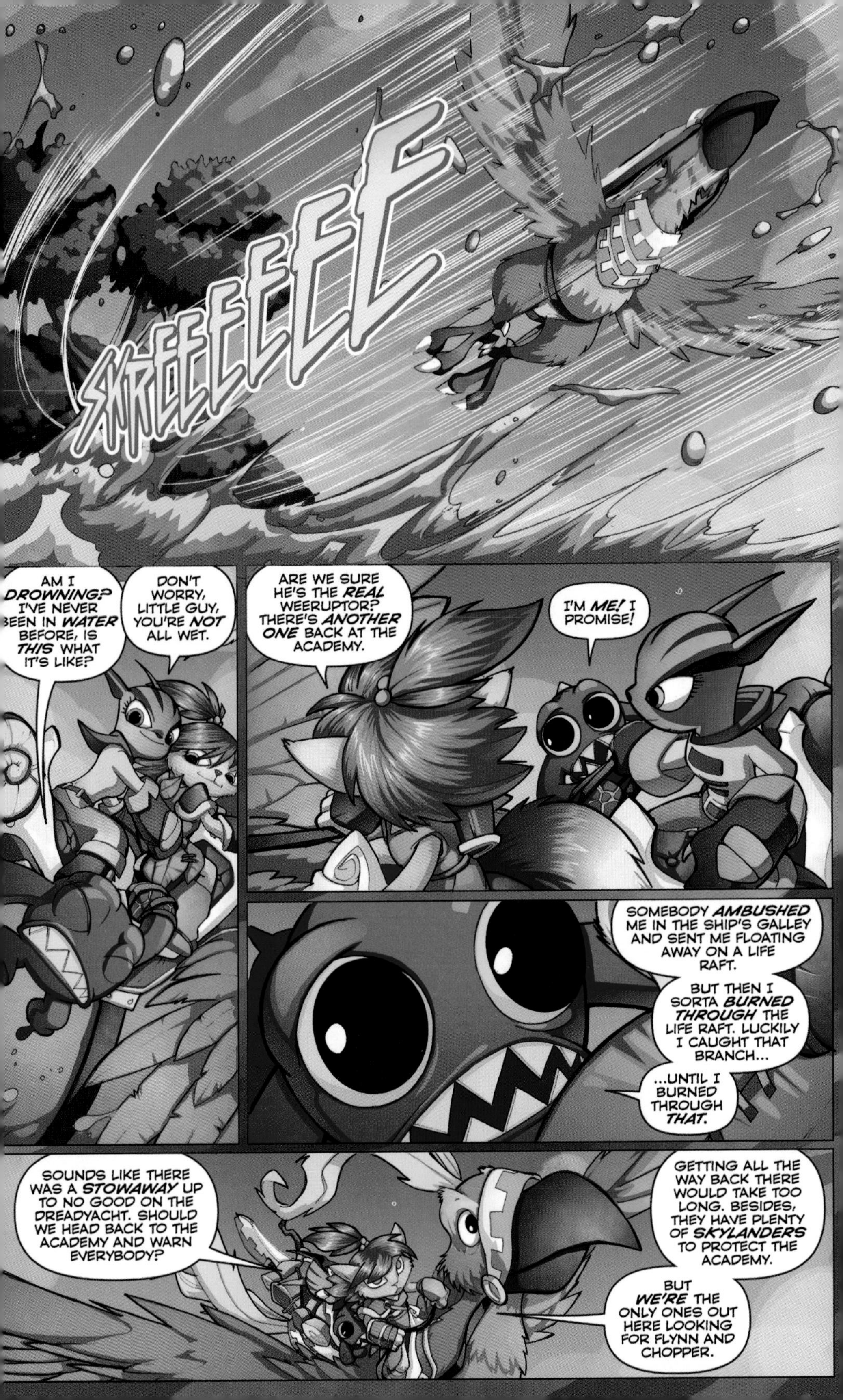
SKREEEEEEE
AM I DROWNING? I'VE NEVER BEEN IN WATER BEFORE, IS THIS WHAT IT'S LIKE?
DON'T WORRY, LITTLE GUY, YOU'RE NOT ALL WET.
ARE WE SURE HE'S THE REAL WEERUPTOR? THERE'S ANOTHER ONE BACK AT THE ACADEMY.
I'M ME! I PROMISE!
SOMEBODY AMBUSHED ME IN THE SHIP'S GALLEY AND SENT ME FLOATING AWAY ON A LIFE RAFT.
BUT THEN I SORTA BURNED THROUGH THE LIFE RAFT. LUCKILY I CAUGHT THAT BRANCH...
...UNTIL I BURNED THROUGH THAT.
SOUNDS LIKE THERE WAS A STOWAWAY UP TO NO GOOD ON THE DREADYACHT. SHOULD WE HEAD BACK TO THE ACADEMY AND WARN EVERYBODY?
GETTING ALL THE WAY BACK THERE WOULD TAKE TOO LONG. BESIDES, THEY HAVE PLENTY OF SKYLANDERS TO PROTECT THE ACADEMY.
BUT WE'RE THE ONLY ONES OUT HERE LOOKING FOR FLYNN AND CHOPPER.

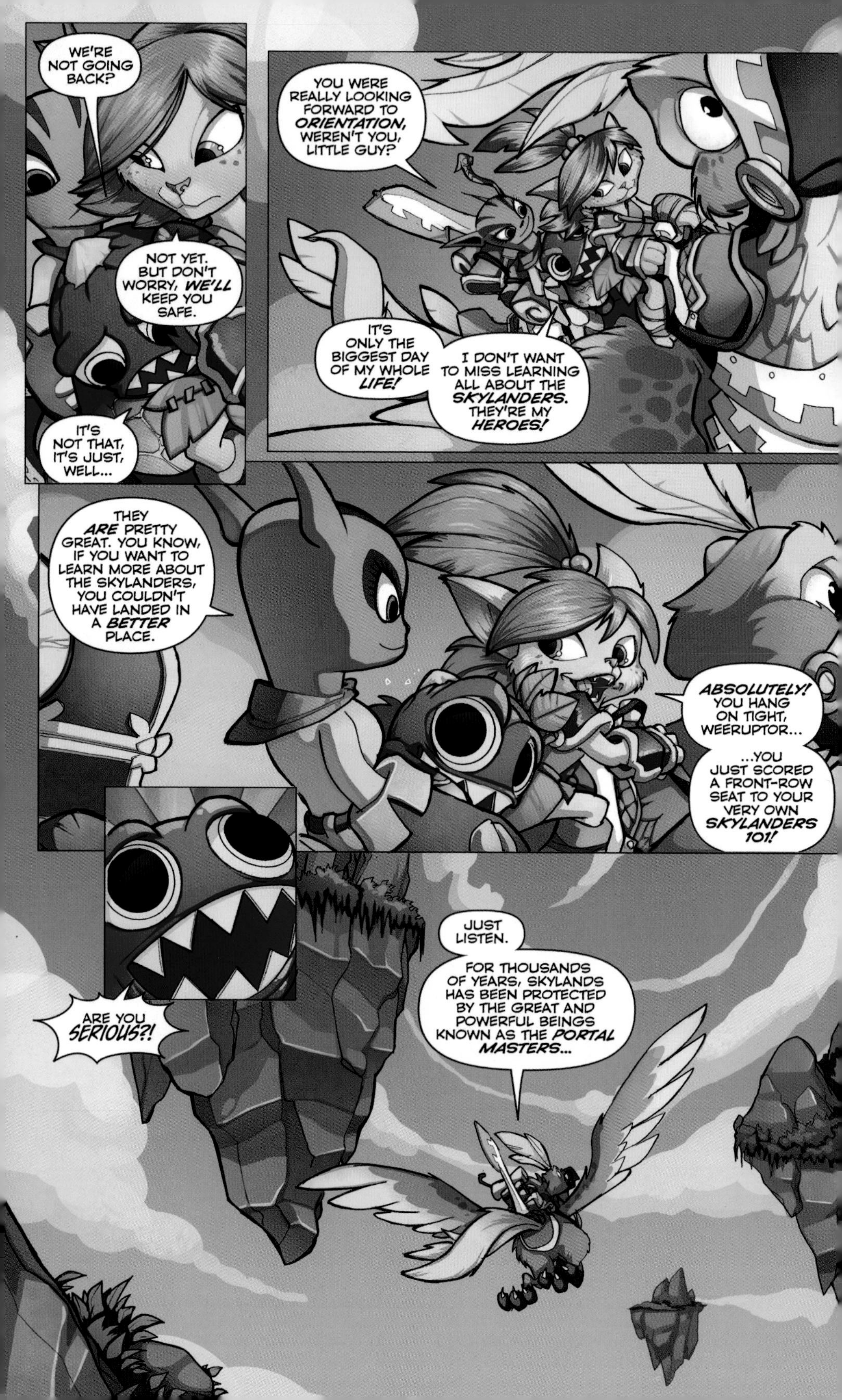
WE'RE NOT GOING BACK?
NOT YET. BUT DON'T WORRY, WE'LL KEEP YOU SAFE.
IT'S NOT THAT, IT'S JUST, WELL...
YOU WERE REALLY LOOKING FORWARD TO ORIENTATION, WEREN'T YOU, LITTLE GUY?
IT'S ONLY THE BIGGEST DAY OF MY WHOLE LIFE!
I DON'T WANT TO MISS LEARNING ALL ABOUT THE SKYLANDERS. THEY'RE MY HEROES!
THEY ARE PRETTY GREAT. YOU KNOW, IF YOU WANT TO LEARN MORE ABOUT THE SKYLANDERS, YOU COULDN'T HAVE LANDED IN A BETTER PLACE.
ABSOLUTELY! YOU HANG ON TIGHT, WEERUPTOR...
...YOU JUST SCORED A FRONT-ROW SEAT TO YOUR VERY OWN SKYLANDERS 101!
ARE YOU SERIOUS?!
JUST LISTEN.
FOR THOUSANDS OF YEARS, SKYLANDS HAS BEEN PROTECTED BY THE GREAT AND POWERFUL BEINGS KNOWN AS THE PORTAL MASTERS...

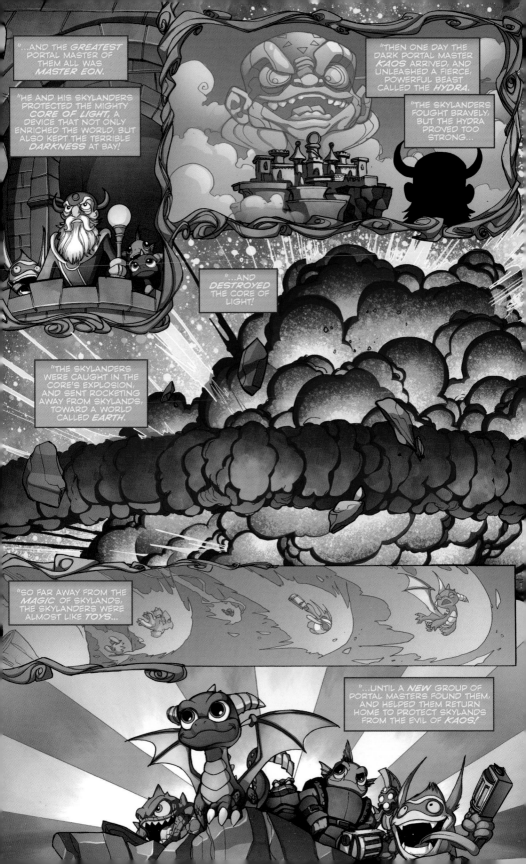

"...AND THE *GREATEST* PORTAL MASTER OF THEM ALL WAS *MASTER EON.*

"HE AND HIS SKYLANDERS PROTECTED THE MIGHTY *CORE OF LIGHT,* A DEVICE THAT NOT ONLY ENRICHED THE WORLD, BUT ALSO KEPT THE TERRIBLE *DARKNESS* AT BAY!

"THEN ONE DAY THE DARK PORTAL MASTER *KAOS* ARRIVED, AND UNLEASHED A FIERCE, POWERFUL BEAST CALLED THE *HYDRA.*

"THE SKYLANDERS FOUGHT BRAVELY, BUT THE HYDRA PROVED TOO STRONG...

"...AND *DESTROYED* THE CORE OF LIGHT!

"THE SKYLANDERS WERE CAUGHT IN THE CORE'S EXPLOSION, AND SENT ROCKETING AWAY FROM SKYLANDS, TOWARD A WORLD CALLED *EARTH.*

"SO FAR AWAY FROM THE *MAGIC* OF SKYLANDS, THE SKYLANDERS WERE ALMOST LIKE *TOYS...*

"...UNTIL A *NEW* GROUP OF PORTAL MASTERS FOUND THEM, AND HELPED THEM RETURN HOME TO PROTECT SKYLANDS FROM THE EVIL OF *KAOS!*

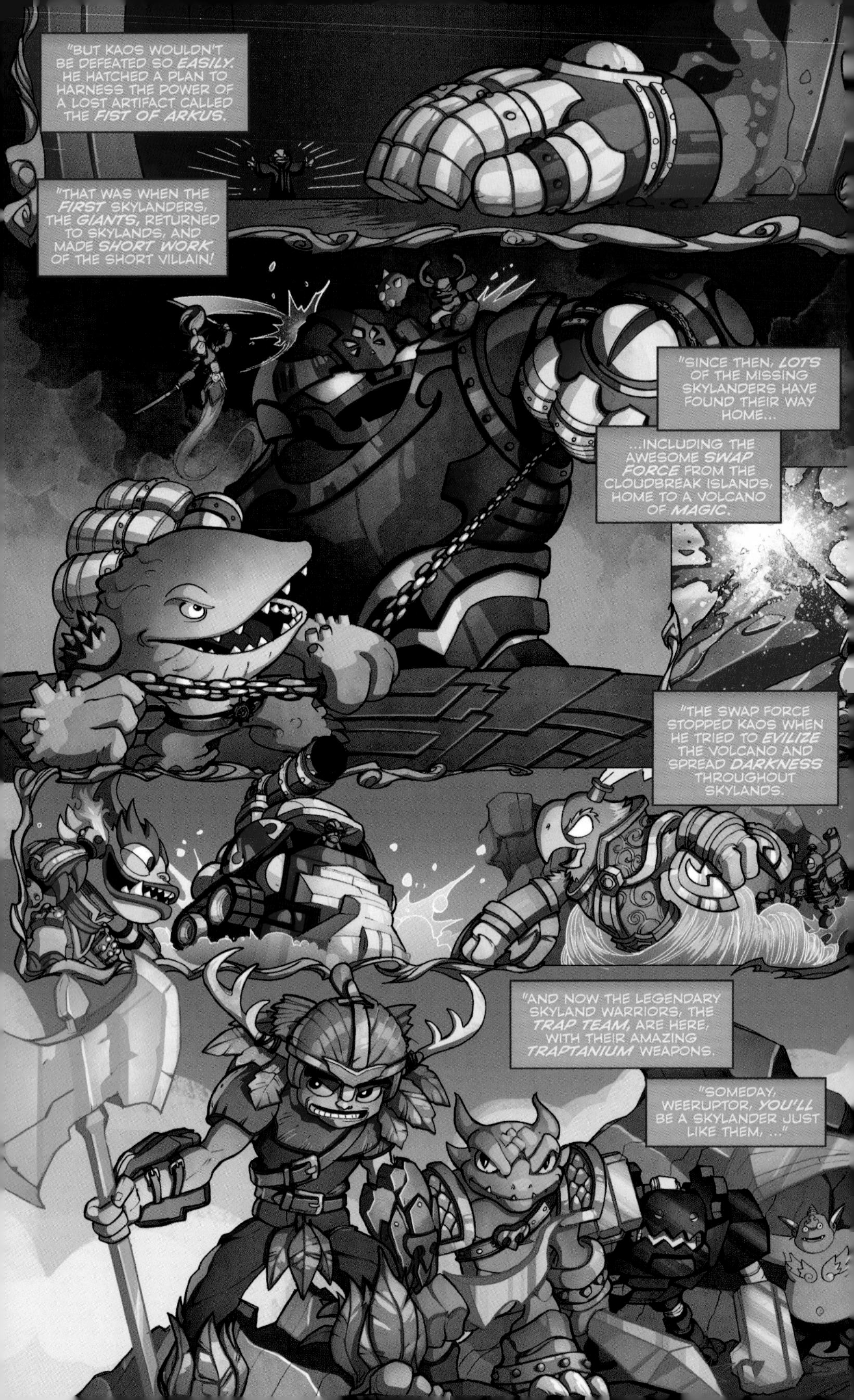
"BUT KAOS WOULDN'T BE DEFEATED SO EASILY. HE HATCHED A PLAN TO HARNESS THE POWER OF A LOST ARTIFACT CALLED THE FIST OF ARKUS.
"THAT WAS WHEN THE FIRST SKYLANDERS, THE GIANTS, RETURNED TO SKYLANDS, AND MADE SHORT WORK OF THE SHORT VILLAIN!
"SINCE THEN, LOTS OF THE MISSING SKYLANDERS HAVE FOUND THEIR WAY HOME...
...INCLUDING THE AWESOME SWAP FORCE FROM THE CLOUDBREAK ISLANDS, HOME TO A VOLCANO OF MAGIC.
"THE SWAP FORCE STOPPED KAOS WHEN HE TRIED TO EVILIZE THE VOLCANO AND SPREAD DARKNESS THROUGHOUT SKYLANDS.
"AND NOW THE LEGENDARY SKYLAND WARRIORS, THE TRAP TEAM, ARE HERE, WITH THEIR AMAZING TRAPTANIUM WEAPONS.
"SOMEDAY, WEERUPTOR, YOU'LL BE A SKYLANDER JUST LIKE THEM, ..."

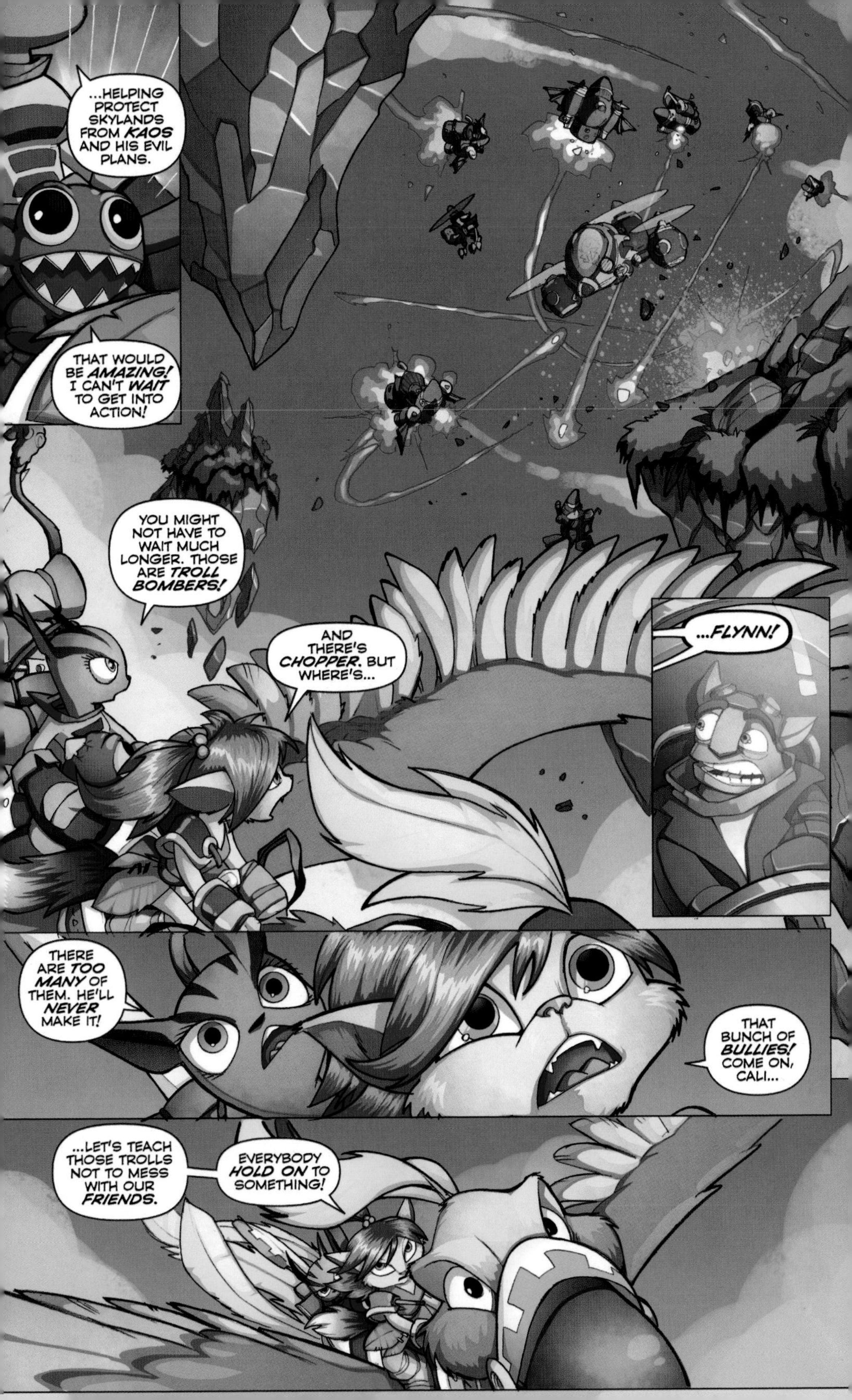
...HELPING PROTECT SKYLANDS FROM KAOS AND HIS EVIL PLANS.
THAT WOULD BE AMAZING! I CAN'T WAIT TO GET INTO ACTION!
YOU MIGHT NOT HAVE TO WAIT MUCH LONGER. THOSE ARE TROLL BOMBERS!
AND THERE'S CHOPPER. BUT WHERE'S...
...FLYNN!
THERE ARE TOO MANY OF THEM. HE'LL NEVER MAKE IT!
THAT BUNCH OF BULLIES! COME ON, CALI...
...LET'S TEACH THOSE TROLLS NOT TO MESS WITH OUR FRIENDS.
EVERYBODY HOLD ON TO SOMETHING!

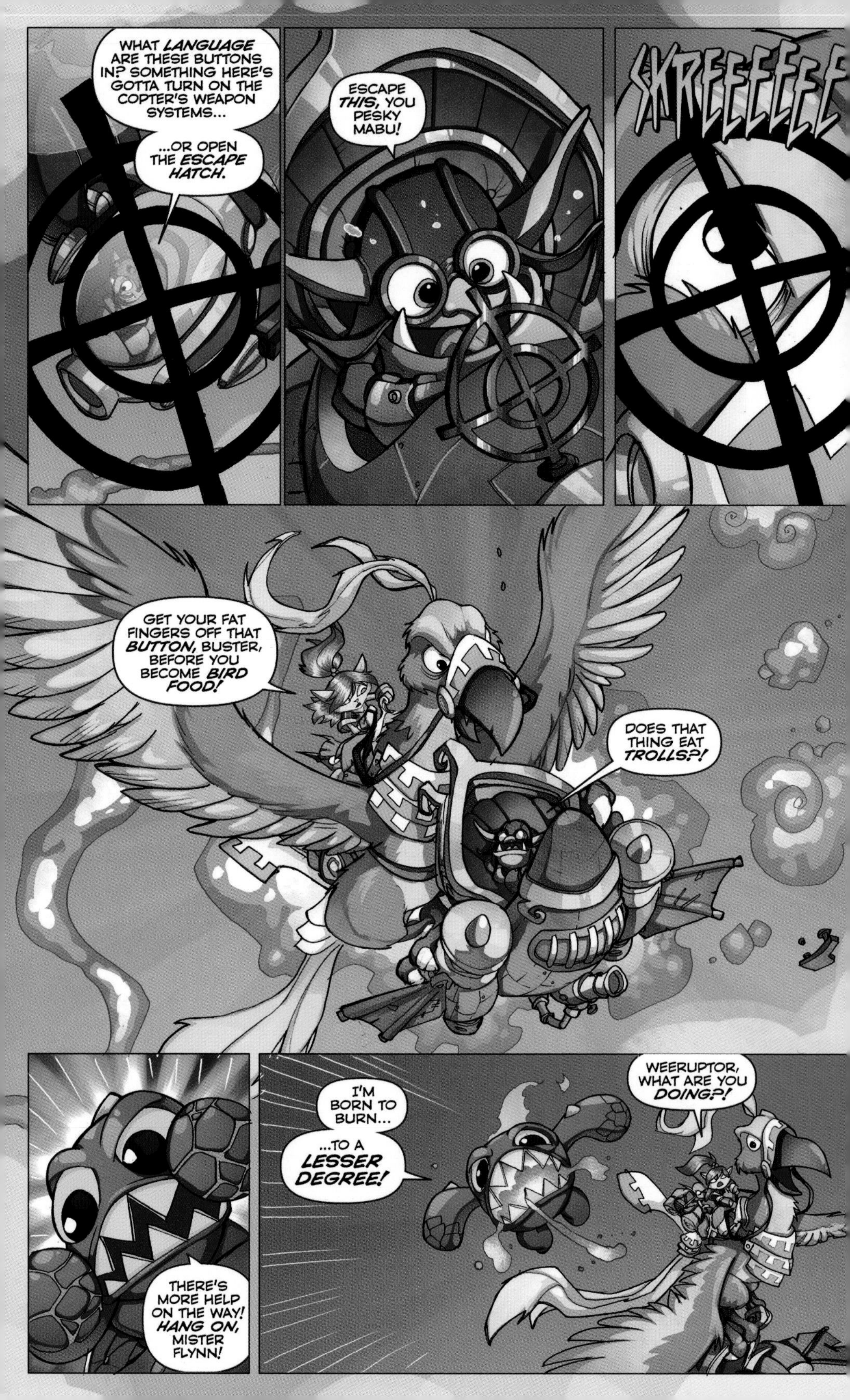
WHAT LANGUAGE ARE THESE BUTTONS IN? SOMETHING HERE'S GOTTA TURN ON THE COPTER'S WEAPON SYSTEMS...
...OR OPEN THE ESCAPE HATCH.
ESCAPE THIS, YOU PESKY MABU!
SKREEEEEE
GET YOUR FAT FINGERS OFF THAT BUTTON, BUSTER, BEFORE YOU BECOME BIRD FOOD!
DOES THAT THING EAT TROLLS?!
THERE'S MORE HELP ON THE WAY! HANG ON, MISTER FLYNN!
I'M BORN TO BURN...
...TO A LESSER DEGREE!
WEERUPTOR, WHAT ARE YOU DOING?!

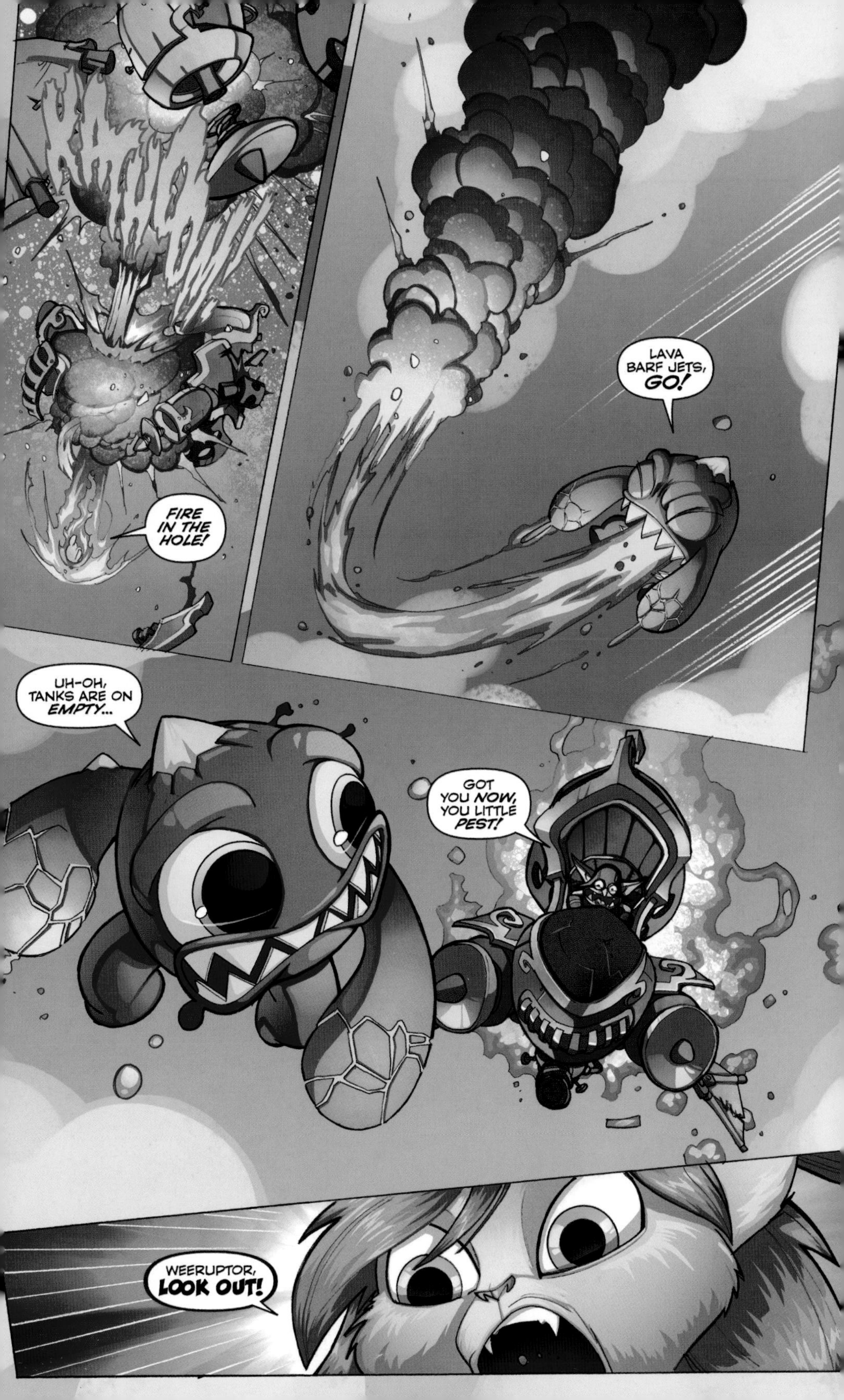
FIRE IN THE HOLE!
LAVA BARF JETS, GO!
UH-OH, TANKS ARE ON EMPTY...
GOT YOU NOW, YOU LITTLE PEST!
WEERUPTOR, LOOK OUT!

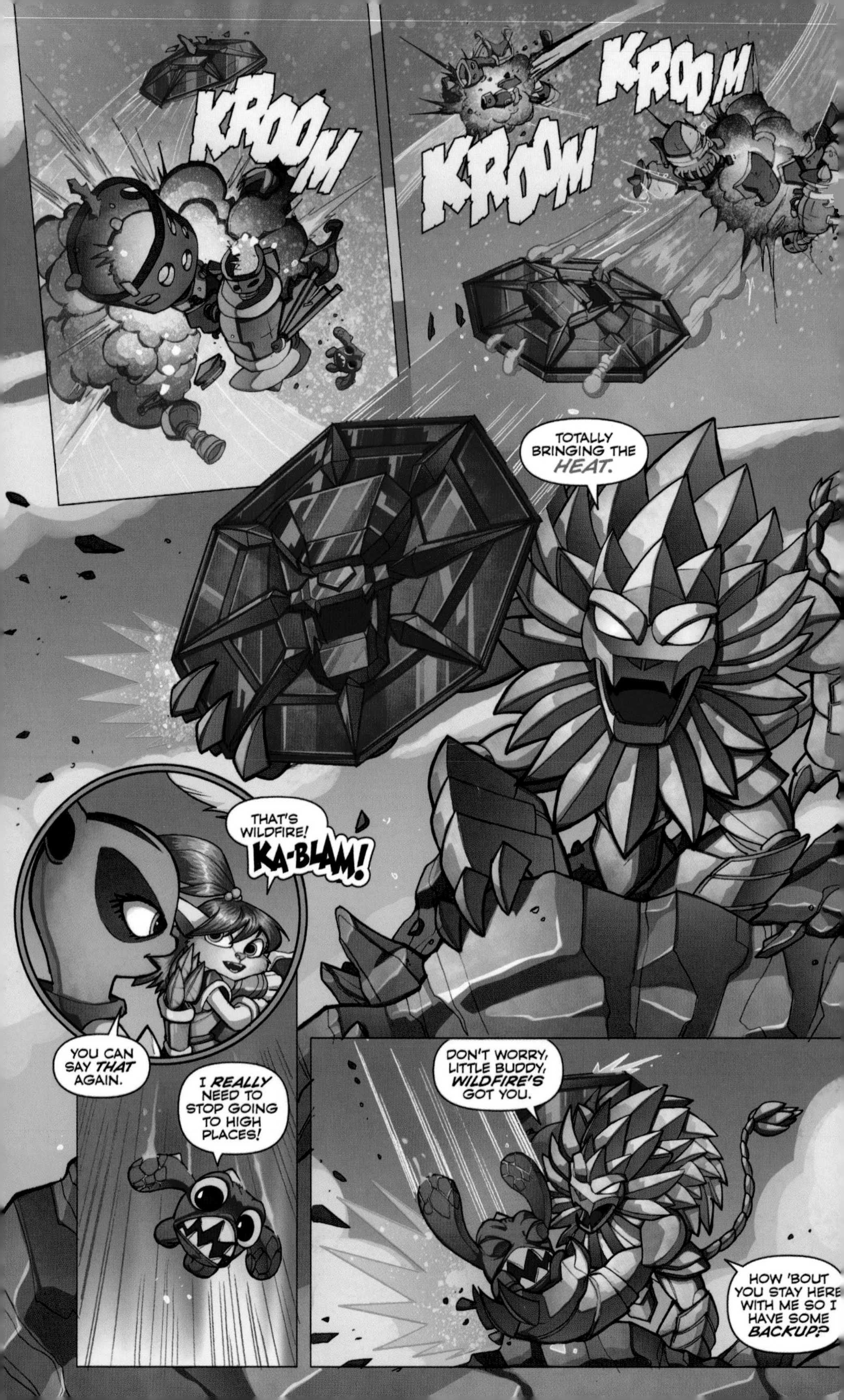
KROOM
KROOM
KROOM
TOTALLY BRINGING THE HEAT.
THAT'S WILDFIRE!
KA-BLAM!
YOU CAN SAY THAT AGAIN.
I REALLY NEED TO STOP GOING TO HIGH PLACES!
DON'T WORRY, LITTLE BUDDY, WILDFIRE'S GOT YOU.
HOW 'BOUT YOU STAY HERE WITH ME SO I HAVE SOME BACKUP?

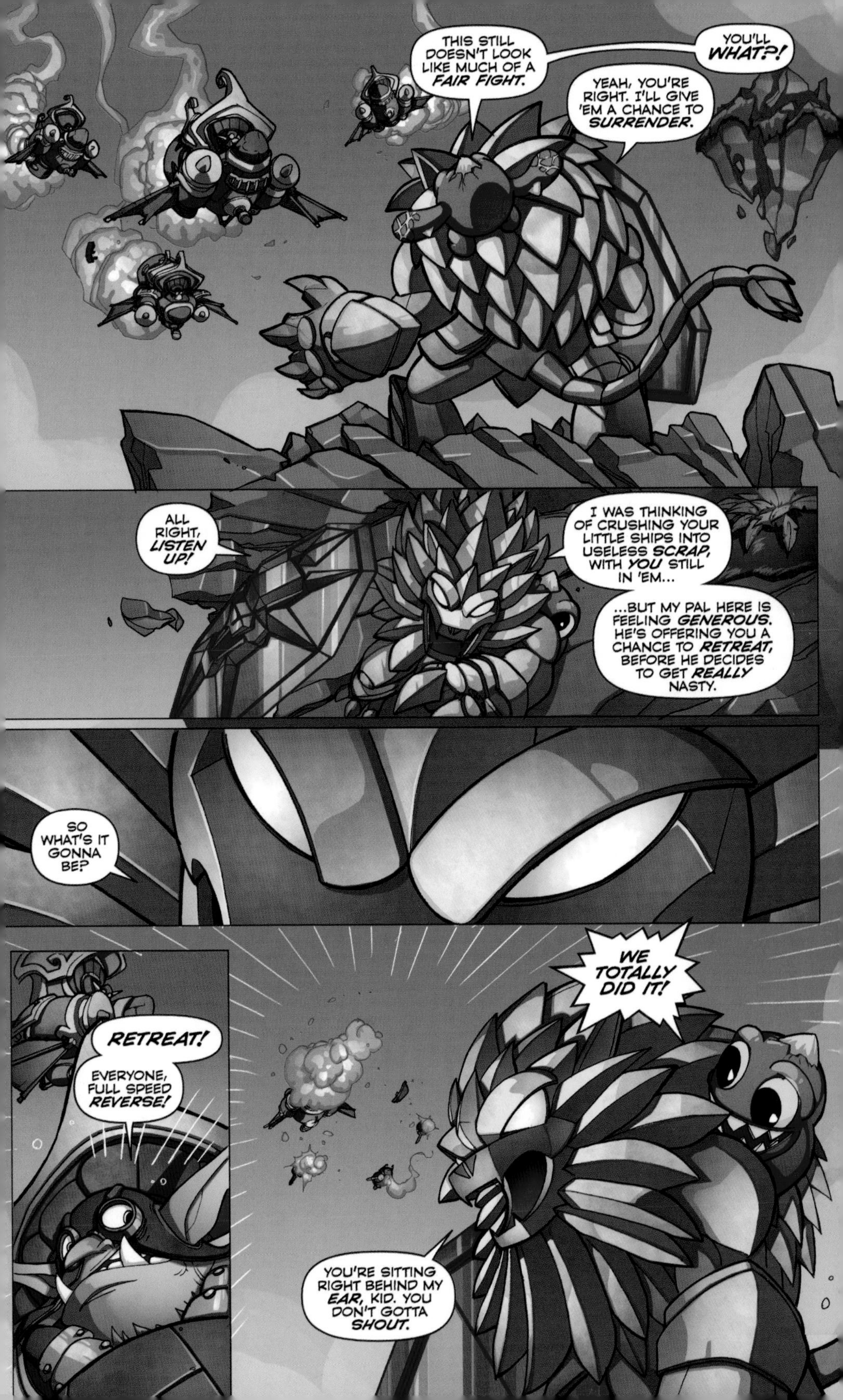
THIS STILL DOESN'T LOOK LIKE MUCH OF A FAIR FIGHT.
YEAH, YOU'RE RIGHT. I'LL GIVE 'EM A CHANCE TO SURRENDER.
YOU'LL WHAT?!
ALL RIGHT, LISTEN UP!
I WAS THINKING OF CRUSHING YOUR LITTLE SHIPS INTO USELESS SCRAP, WITH YOU STILL IN 'EM...
...BUT MY PAL HERE IS FEELING GENEROUS. HE'S OFFERING YOU A CHANCE TO RETREAT, BEFORE HE DECIDES TO GET REALLY NASTY.
SO WHAT'S IT GONNA BE?
RETREAT!
EVERYONE, FULL SPEED REVERSE!
WE TOTALLY DID IT!
YOU'RE SITTING RIGHT BEHIND MY EAR, KID. YOU DON'T GOTTA SHOUT.

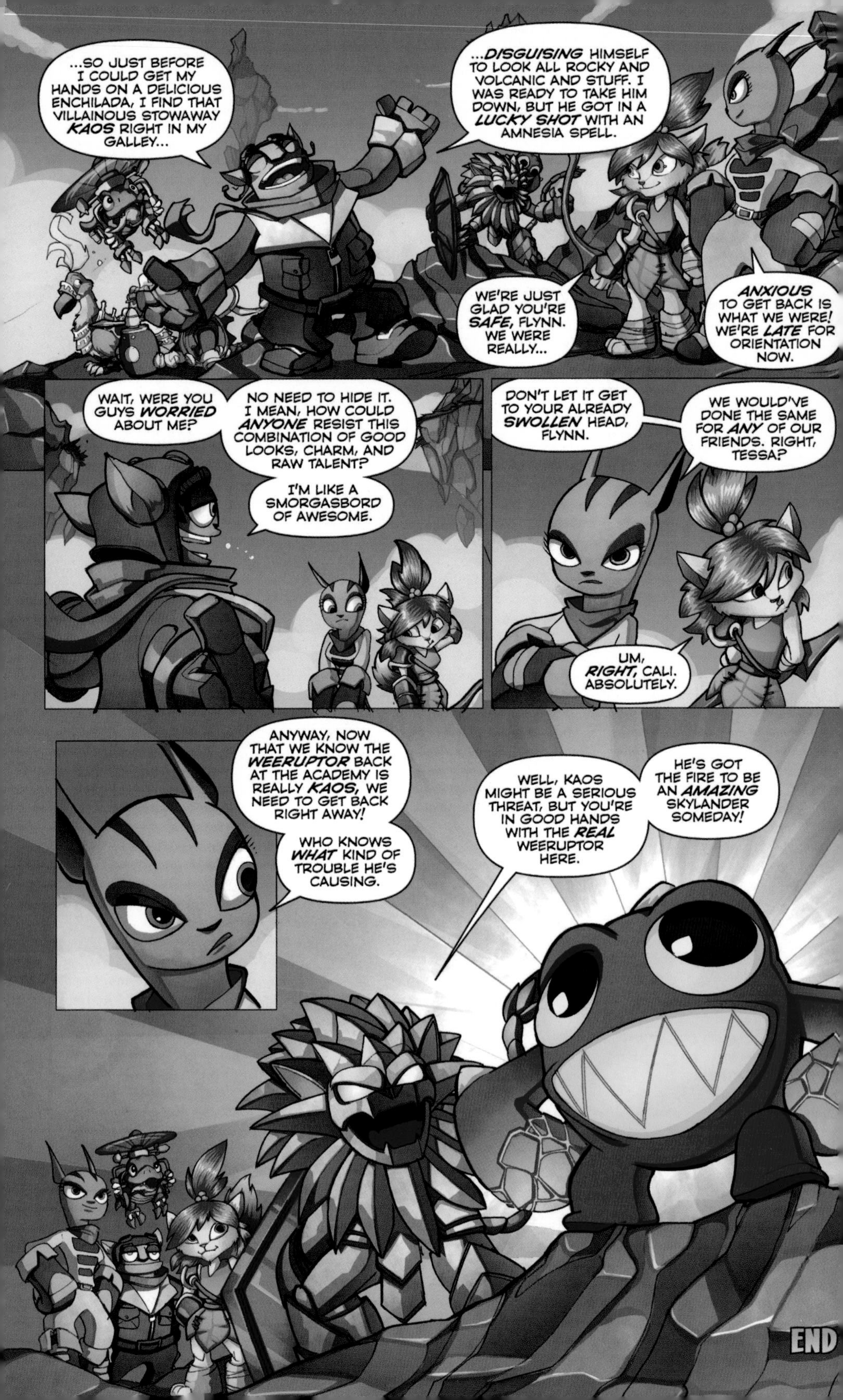
...SO JUST BEFORE I COULD GET MY HANDS ON A DELICIOUS ENCHILADA, I FIND THAT VILLAINOUS STOWAWAY KAOS RIGHT IN MY GALLEY...
...DISGUISING HIMSELF TO LOOK ALL ROCKY AND VOLCANIC AND STUFF. I WAS READY TO TAKE HIM DOWN, BUT HE GOT IN A LUCKY SHOT WITH AN AMNESIA SPELL.
WE'RE JUST GLAD YOU'RE SAFE, FLYNN. WE WERE REALLY...
ANXIOUS TO GET BACK IS WHAT WE WERE! WE'RE LATE FOR ORIENTATION NOW.
WAIT, WERE YOU GUYS WORRIED ABOUT ME?
NO NEED TO HIDE IT. I MEAN, HOW COULD ANYONE RESIST THIS COMBINATION OF GOOD LOOKS, CHARM, AND RAW TALENT?
I'M LIKE A SMORGASBORD OF AWESOME.
DON'T LET IT GET TO YOUR ALREADY SWOLLEN HEAD, FLYNN.
WE WOULD'VE DONE THE SAME FOR ANY OF OUR FRIENDS. RIGHT, TESSA?
UM, RIGHT, CALI. ABSOLUTELY.
ANYWAY, NOW THAT WE KNOW THE WEERUPTOR BACK AT THE ACADEMY IS REALLY KAOS, WE NEED TO GET BACK RIGHT AWAY!
WHO KNOWS WHAT KIND OF TROUBLE HE'S CAUSING.
WELL, KAOS MIGHT BE A SERIOUS THREAT, BUT YOU'RE IN GOOD HANDS WITH THE REAL WEERUPTOR HERE.
HE'S GOT THE FIRE TO BE AN AMAZING SKYLANDER SOMEDAY!
END

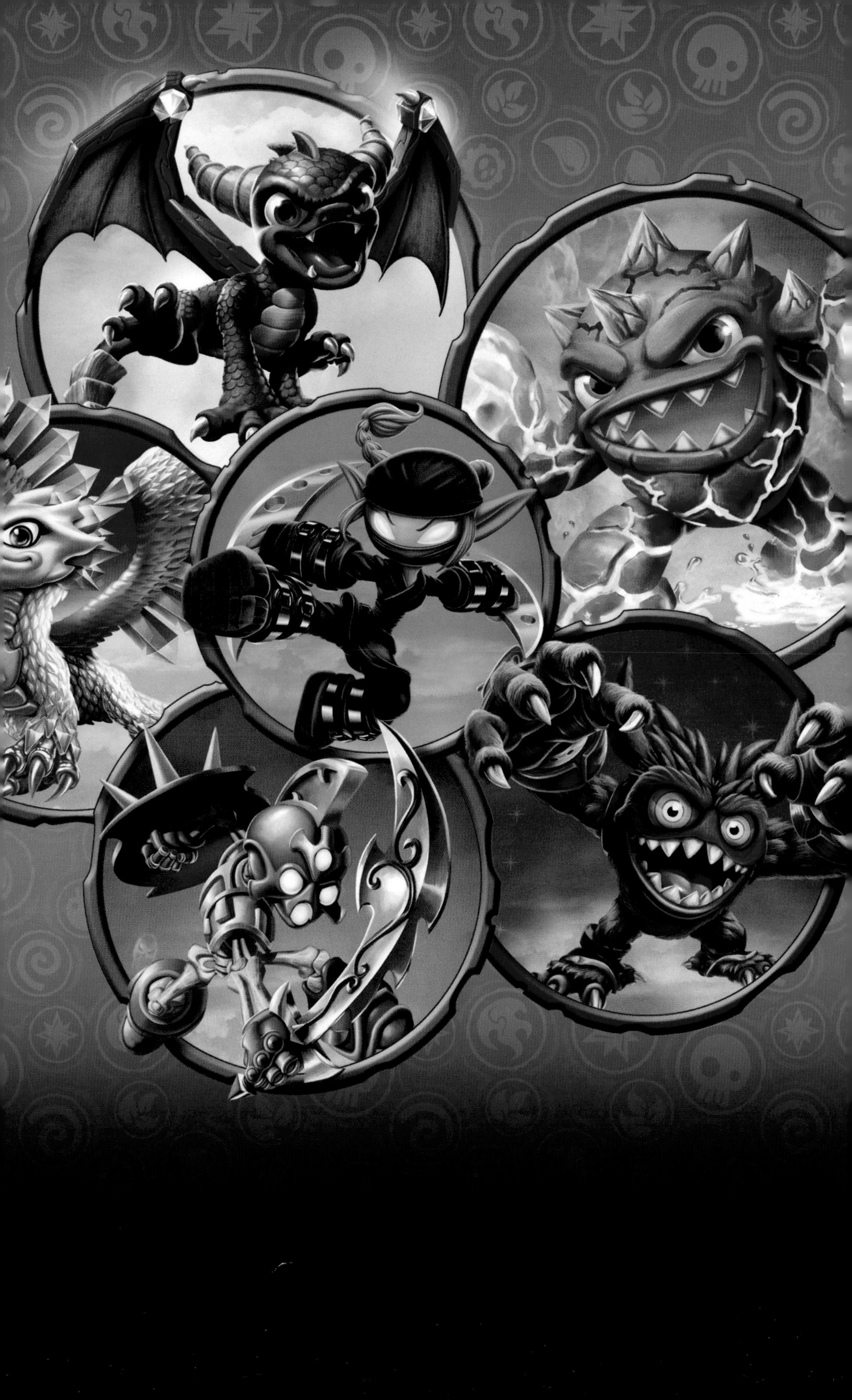

FOOD FIGHT

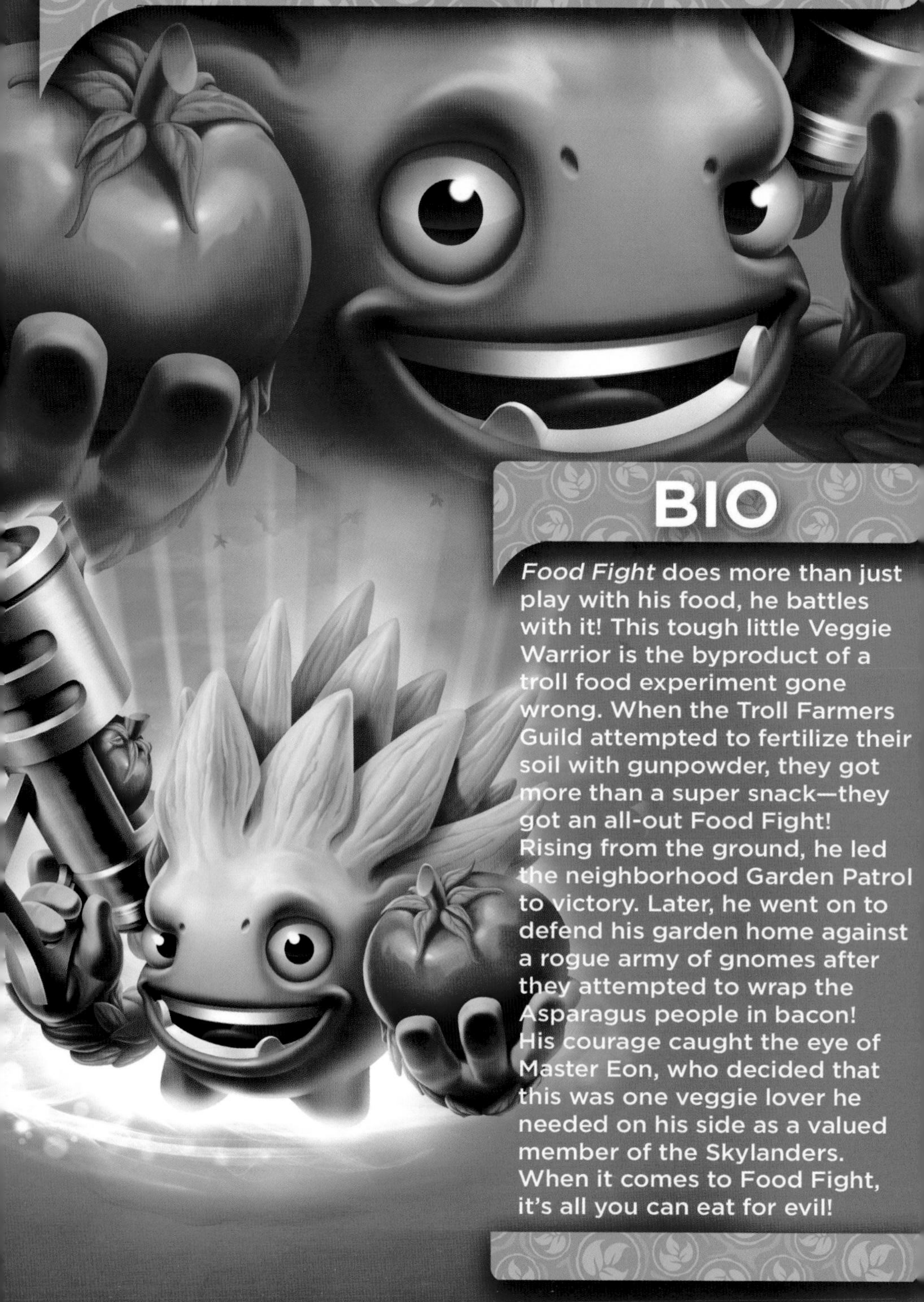

BIO

Food Fight does more than just play with his food, he battles with it! This tough little Veggie Warrior is the byproduct of a troll food experiment gone wrong. When the Troll Farmers Guild attempted to fertilize their soil with gunpowder, they got more than a super snack—they got an all-out Food Fight! Rising from the ground, he led the neighborhood Garden Patrol to victory. Later, he went on to defend his garden home against a rogue army of gnomes after they attempted to wrap the Asparagus people in bacon! His courage caught the eye of Master Eon, who decided that this was one veggie lover he needed on his side as a valued member of the Skylanders. When it comes to Food Fight, it's all you can eat for evil!

WILDFIRE

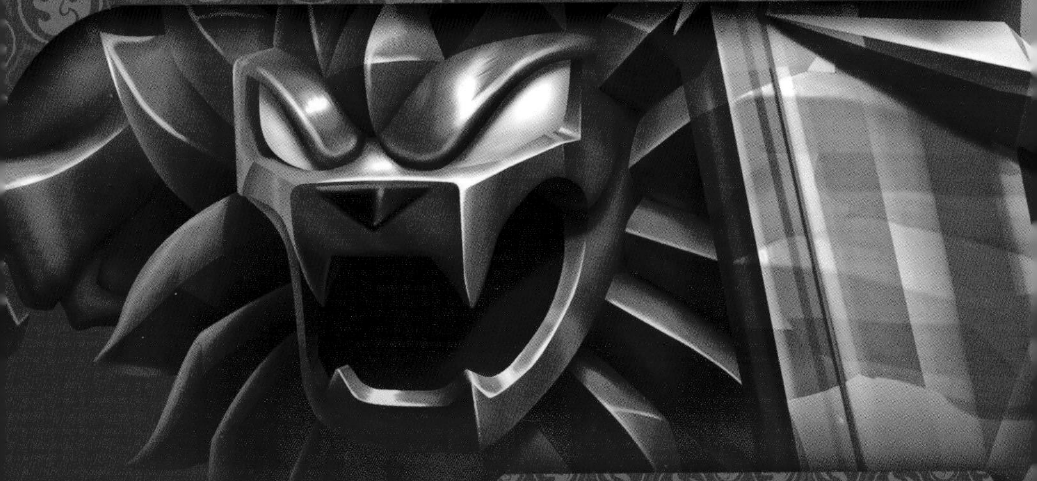

BIO

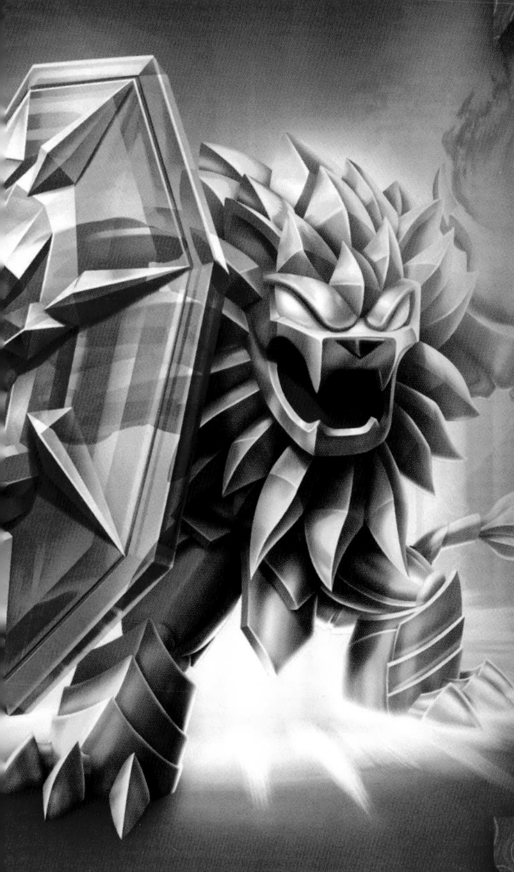

Wildfire was once a young lion of the Fire Claw Clan, about to enter into the Rite of Infernos—a test of survival in the treacherous fire plains. However, because he was made of gold, he was treated as an outcast and not allowed to participate. But this didn't stop him. That night, Wildfire secretly followed the path of the other lions, carrying only his father's enchanted shield. Soon he found them cornered by a giant flame scorpion. Using the shield, he protected the group from the beast's enormous stinging tail, giving them time to safely escape. And though Wildfire was injured in the fight, his father's shield magically changed him—magnifying the strength that was already in his heart—making him the mightiest of his clan. Now part of the Trap Team, Wildfire uses his enormous Traptanium-bonded shield to defend any and all who need it!

SNAP SHOT

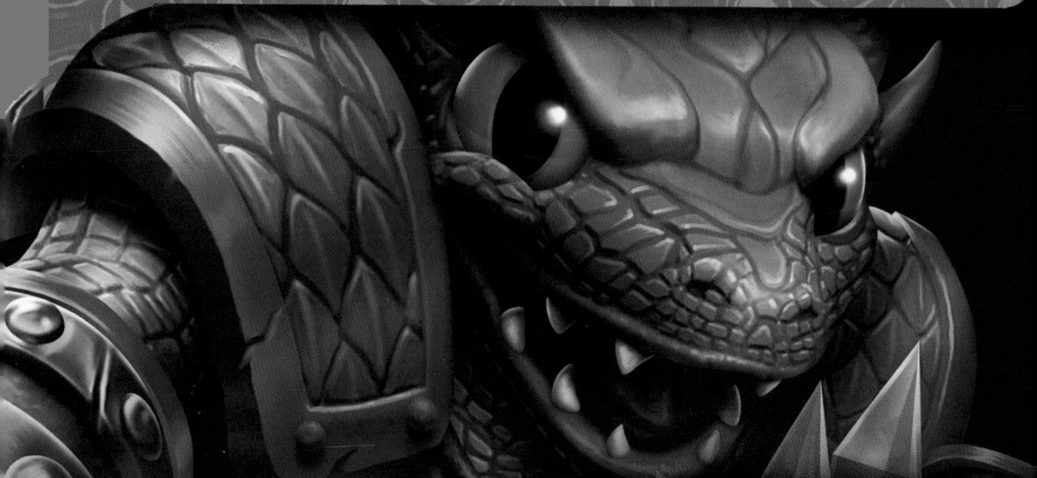

BIO

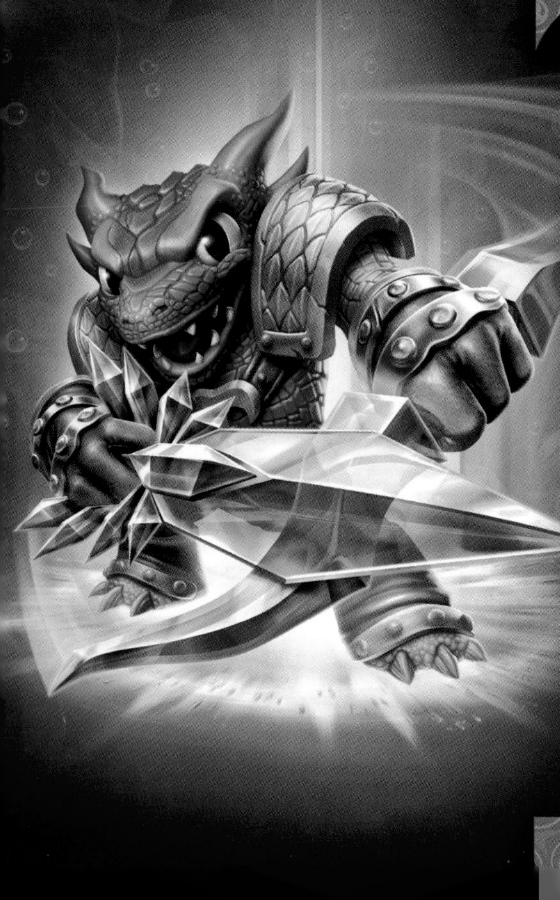

Snap Shot came from a long line of Crocagators that lived in the remote Swamplands, where he hunted chompies for sport. After rounding up every evil critter in his homeland, Snap Shot ventured out into the world to learn new techniques that he could use to track down more challenging monsters. He journeyed far and wide, perfecting his archery skills with the Elves and his hunting skills with the wolves. Soon he was the most revered monster hunter in Skylands—a reputation that caught the attention of Master Eon. It then wasn't long before Snap Shot became the leader of the Trap Masters, a fearless team of Skylanders that mastered legendary weapons made of pure Traptanium. It was this elite team that tracked down and captured the most notorious villains Skylands had ever known!

WALLOP

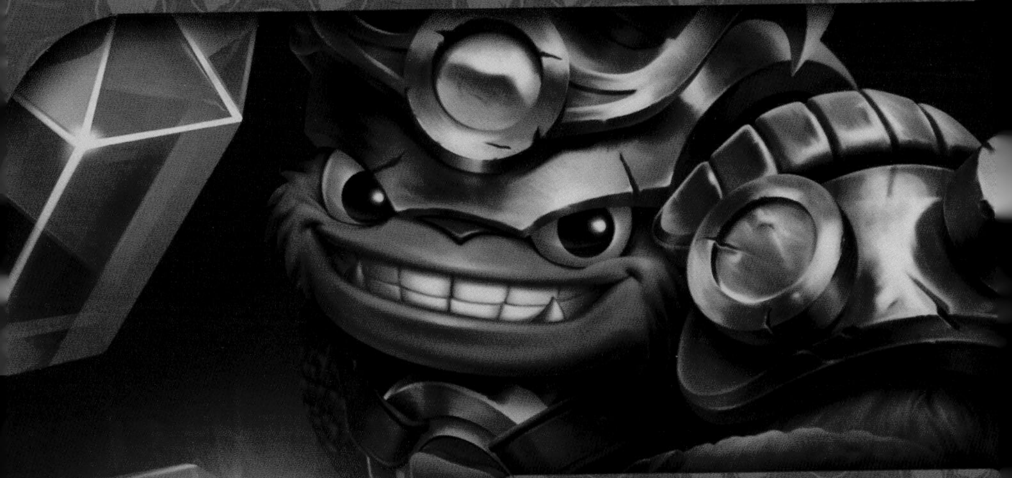

BIO

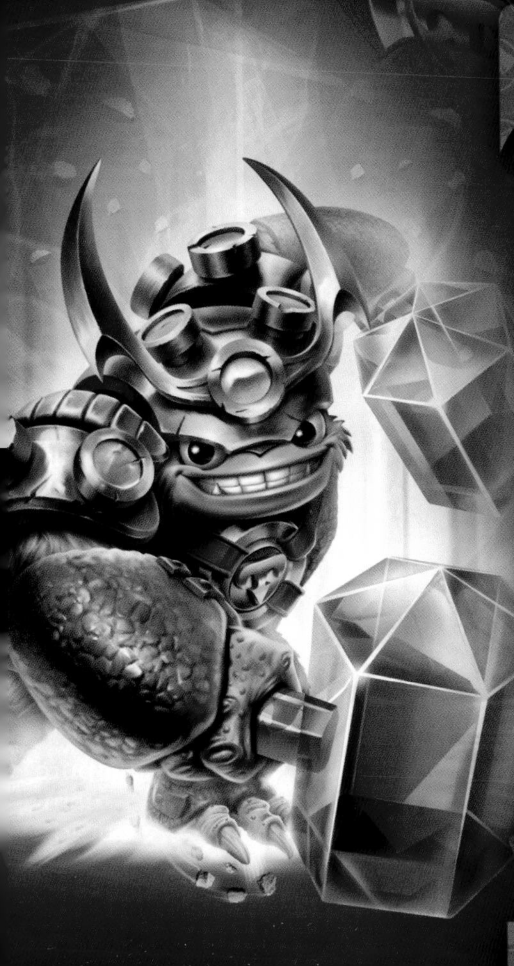

For generations, *Wallop's* people used the volcanic lava pits of Mount Scorch to forge the most awesome weapons in all of Skylands. And Wallop was the finest apprentice any of the masters had ever seen. Using hammers in both of his mighty hands, he could tirelessly pound and shape the incredibly hot metal into the sharpest swords or the hardest axes. But on the day he was to demonstrate his skills to the masters of his craft, a fierce fire viper awoke from his deep sleep in the belly of the volcano. The huge snake erupted forth, attacking Wallop's village. But by bravely charging the beast with his two massive hammers, Wallop was able to bring down the creature and save his village. Now with his Traptanium-infused hammers, he fights with the Skylanders to protect the lands from any evil that rises to attack!

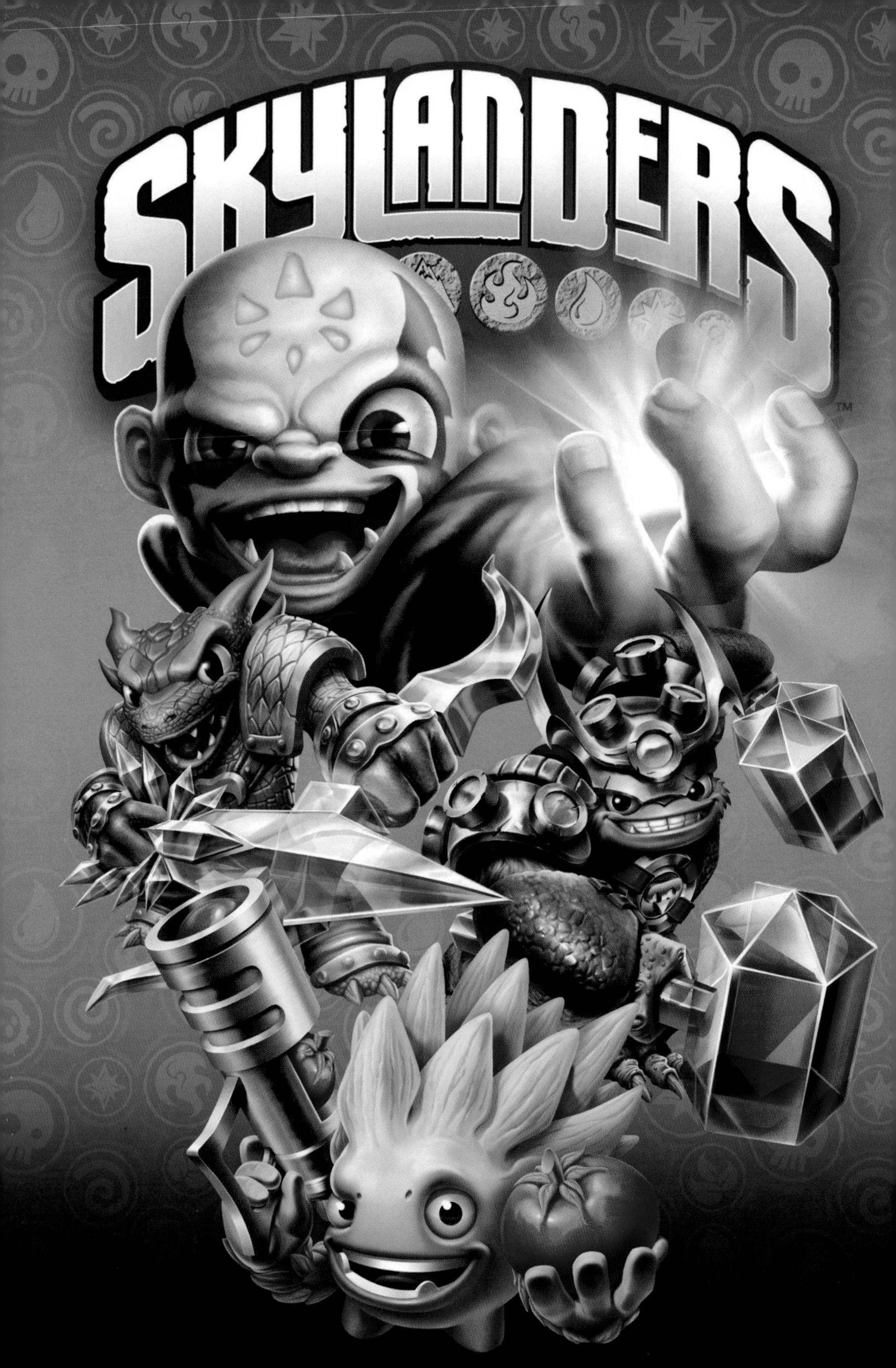
SKYLANDERS™

THE KAOS TRAP